Walt Disney's Peter Pan

Illustrated by the Disney Storybook Artists
Adapted by Kate Hannigan

Published by
Louis Weber, C.E.O.
Publications International, Ltd.
7373 North Cicero Avenue
Lincolnwood, Illinois 60712

Ground Floor, 59 Gloucester Place
London W1U 8JJ

Customer Service: 1-800-595-8484 or customer_service@pilbooks.com

www.pilbooks.com

p i kids is a registered trademark of Publications International, Ltd.

Manufactured in China.

ISBN-10: 0-7853-9539-3
ISBN-13: 978-0-7853-9539-3

In a corner house on a quiet street in London lived three children, Wendy, John, and Michael Darling. The children loved to tell stories of the brave Peter Pan and a magical place called Never Land.

Their mother believed Peter Pan was the spirit of youth. Wendy, John, and Michael believed Peter Pan was a real person, and they made him the hero of their games.

"Peter Pan to the rescue!" the boys would shout in their pretend sword fights.

Peter Pan liked to visit the Darling's house. The children believed in him. He would sit outside the nursery window and listen to Wendy tell wonderful stories about him.

"Peter Pan? Poppycock!" said Wendy's father. He was tired of Wendy's wild stories and said it was time she moved into her own room. It was to be her last night in the nursery with her little brothers.

"Sooner or later, people have to grow up," Father said. But Wendy didn't want to grow up.

When the children fell asleep that night, Peter Pan and
Tinker Bell sneaked into the house. They were searching
for Peter's shadow. Peter and Tinker Bell looked all over
the room. Finally, Peter went to the dresser and opened
the top drawer. Out jumped his shadow. He chased it
around the room until he woke up Wendy.

She was excited to see Peter Pan. She pulled out a
needle and thread and sewed the shadow to the tips of
Peter's toes. This way, Peter Pan would never lose his
shadow again.

Peter was very upset to hear it would be Wendy's last night in the nursery. He wanted to whisk her off to Never Land, where no one ever had to grow up.

Wendy and her brothers wondered how they could get to Never Land. Peter said they would fly there, of course. And with a sprinkling of pixie dust from Tinker Bell, they were ready. "Come on, everybody!" he said. "We're off to Never Land!"

Peter Pan led the way as he, Wendy, John, and Michael soared over the city of London. They flew high above the rooftops among the clouds, on and on to Never Land.

Waiting for Peter Pan in the waters off Never Land was a pirate ship commanded by the terrible Captain Hook. He wanted to find Peter's hideaway and capture him.

Hook didn't like Peter. But even worse, he despised the crocodile that had sunk his teeth into him in a fight with Peter Pan long ago. Whenever Hook heard a *tick-tock, tick-tock,* he knew the hungry crocodile was lurking somewhere in the water nearby.

When Peter and his friends reached Never Land, they perched on a cloud overlooking the island. Peter pointed out his favorite places, like Mermaid Lagoon.

Suddenly, there was a *bang!* Captain Hook had fired a cannonball right at Peter Pan. Peter told Tinker Bell to take Wendy, John, and Michael to safety with the Lost Boys while he distracted Hook.

Tinker Bell was jealous of Wendy, so she flew too fast for the children to keep up. When she reached the Lost Boys, Tinker Bell told them to try to knock Wendy from the sky.

The Lost Boys hurled stones and wooden swords into the air. Wendy lost her balance and began to tumble to the ground. Just as she was about to crash onto the rocks below, Peter Pan swooped down and rescued her.

Peter was angry and charged Tinker Bell with high treason. "Are you guilty or not guilty?" he asked her.

Tinker Bell was guilty, and Peter Pan banished her from the island forever. Wendy said that was a bit harsh.

"Okay," Peter said, "for a week then."

Once Wendy, John, and Michael were safely on the ground, they were eager to explore Never Land. John and Michael marched off into the woods to play follow the leader with the Lost Boys. And Peter took Wendy to visit Mermaid Lagoon.

As Wendy met the mermaids, Captain Hook paddled by in a small boat with Tiger Lily, an Indian princess. They were headed for Skull Rock. Peter and Wendy followed them to see what they were up to.

Captain Hook had captured Tiger Lily and wanted her to reveal Peter Pan's hideaway. Tiger Lily wouldn't tell Hook anything. Peter wanted to rescue the princess, so he began to play tricks on Hook.

Peter flew into the air, taunting and teasing the captain. They battled up and down Skull Rock, spinning and jumping over the rocks. Peter Pan was too fast for Hook and quickly got the better of him.

Suddenly, Hook heard the familiar sound of *tick-tock, tick-tock*. His eyes bulged, and his teeth chattered. It was the crocodile waiting for him!

Captain Hook splashed into the water, and the crocodile chased him all the way back to his ship. Peter Pan rescued Tiger Lily and returned her to her father, the Indian chief.

Back on his pirate ship, Captain Hook was angrier than
ever. He thought Peter Pan had made a fool of him, so he
devised a plan to get Peter once and for all. Hook heard
that Peter had banished Tinker Bell from Never Land.
"Maybe she can lead us to Peter Pan!" Captain Hook said.

Tinker Bell sat alone in the woods and was miserable.
She missed Peter and the Lost Boys as she watched them
dance around the Indian chief's campfire.

It didn't take long for Captain Hook to capture Tinker
Bell and bring her back to his pirate ship. Hook pretended
to be Tinker Bell's friend and tricked her into showing
him the way to Peter Pan's hiding place. Tinker Bell made
Hook promise not to lay a hand — or a hook — on Peter.

Hook promised, but he was deceitful. After Tinker Bell
showed him the way to the hideout, Hook locked her up
in a glass case.

After the campfire, Wendy, John, and Michael were ready to return home. The Lost Boys were homesick, too.

Peter was sad that they would want to leave Never Land. He wanted them to stay and warned them, "You can go back and grow up. But just remember: Once you go, you can never come back."

Captain Hook and the pirates were waiting in the woods
as the children left Peter's hideway. The pirates captured
all of Peter's friends—Wendy, John, Michael, and the
Lost Boys. Hook took them back to his ship and tried to
make them become pirates. Captain Hook said they could
join up or walk the plank.

"Peter Pan will save us," Wendy said confidently.
Captain Hook and his pirates laughed. They told Wendy
they had left a present for Peter Pan. It was set to explode
at six o'clock—and that was just seconds away!

At the last moment, Tinker Bell escaped and flew to
Peter Pan. She warned him about Captain Hook's plan.

There was a loud bang, and black dust flew everywhere. Peter Pan climbed out of the ashes and looked for Tinker Bell. She had saved his life! Peter called her name and heard the faint tinkling of her bells deep in the rubble.

Peter knew the others needed his help, but he had to save Tinker Bell first. Even though they had argued, Tinker Bell meant more to Peter Pan than anything in the whole world.

Back at Hook's ship, the pirates made Wendy walk the plank. When she reached the end of the board, Wendy closed her eyes and bravely took the final step.

Captain Hook listened for a splash, but he didn't hear
one. He shouted to his pirates, demanding to know what
had happened.

Suddenly Peter Pan flew through the air with Wendy
safely in his arms. He had caught her just before she fell
into the water. Tinker Bell hovered beside them.

"This time you've gone too far, Hook!" Peter shouted.

Peter Pan freed John, Michael, and the Lost Boys, and together they battled the pirates. Peter flew through the air and lunged at Hook. The captain waved his hook and chased Peter Pan up and down the ship.

"Come back here, you coward!" shouted Hook. Peter said nobody called him a coward and got away with it.

After a long and fierce battle, it was clear Peter had beaten Hook. Peter told him he was free to go. But Captain Hook was a cheat, and he made one last lunge at Peter. Hook slipped and fell down, down, down into the water below.

Tick-tock, tick-tock! The crocodile was waiting for him. Snapping its jaws, the crocodile swallowed Captain Hook in one gulp. Hook climbed right back out of its mouth carrying an alarm clock he'd found inside.

The pirates jumped in a rowboat and followed after their captain. Hook disappeared from Never Land, racing through the waters to get away from the hungry crocodile.

Peter Pan set sail on Captain Hook's ship. He understood that his friends wanted to find their way home. With a sprinkling of pixie dust, Tinker Bell turned the ship into gleaming gold, and it soared through the sky back to London.

Wendy's parents opened the nursery door and found the children asleep. Wendy awoke and pointed up at the moon and Peter Pan's pirate ship sailing across it. Her parents stared out the window. Father said he had a strange feeling he'd seen that ship before. He was beginning to believe.